Honk! Honk!
Add lots of
busy cars stuck
in traffic.

Different Diggers

Finish the diggers with scoops, wheels,
caterpillar tracks, and more.

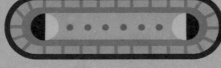

Tough Truck

The truck driver needs to make a delivery this morning.
Use your stickers to finish off the controls.

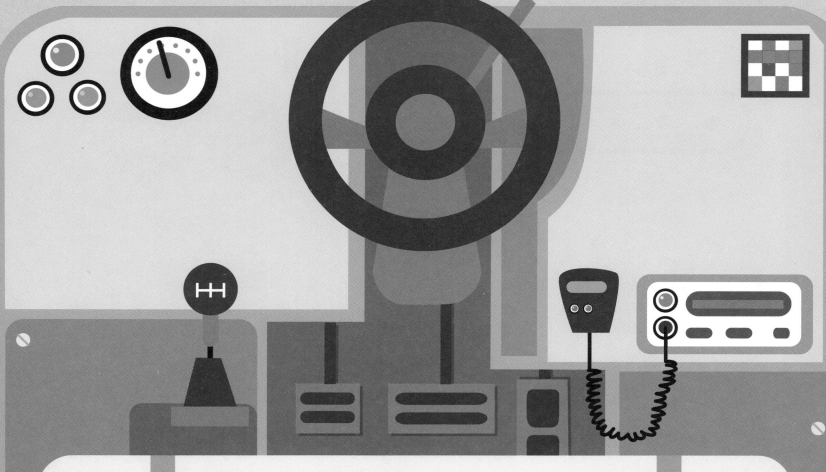

Loading Up

Can you spot five differences between these two pictures?

Add a truck wheel each time you spot a difference.

Down at the Docks

It's a busy day down at the docks. Load up the cargo ship with containers and barrels.

Ahoy there! Fill the water with boats too.

Fill Up the Ferry

The ferry goes back and forth across the harbor all day long.
How many cars can you get safely to the other side?

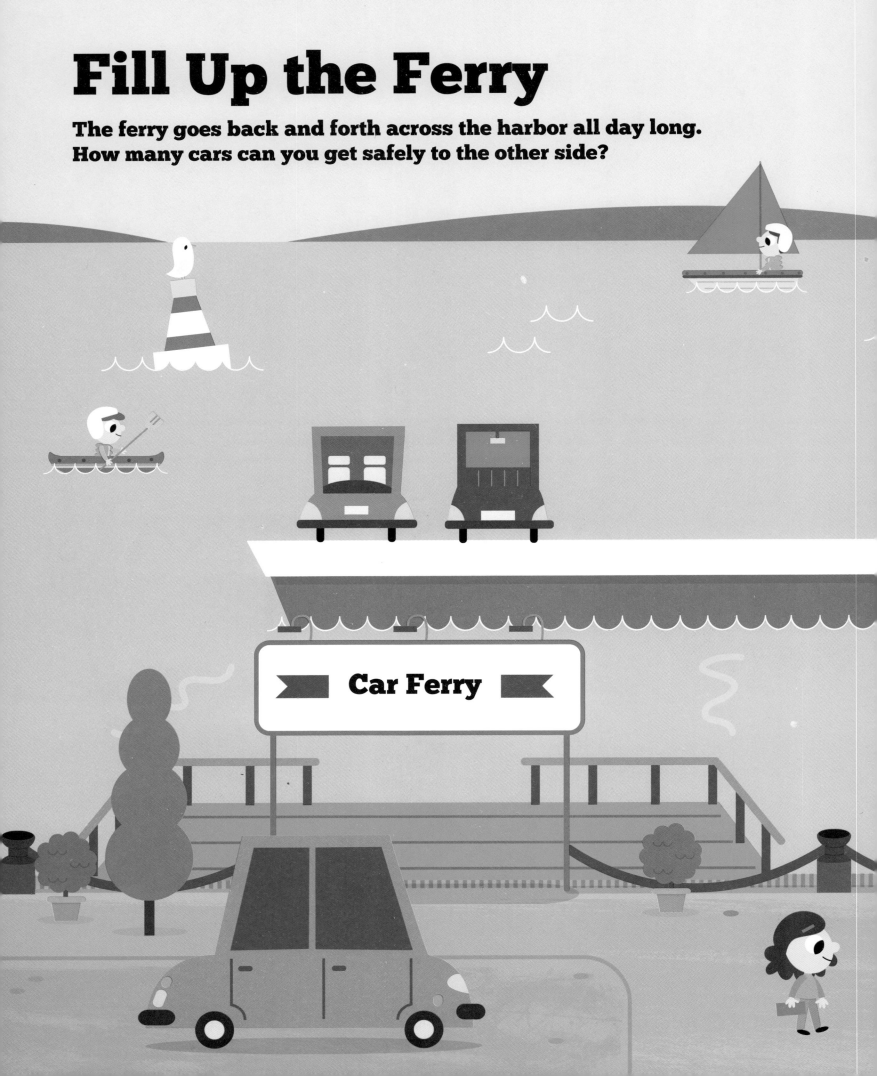

Car Ferry

Busy Buses

It's a busy day, and lots of people are waiting for the bus. Match the numbers to park the buses at the right stops.

Acrobatic Air Show

Lots of excited people have come to see the air show. Use your plane stickers to make an exciting display for the crowd.

Can you see the plane doing an acrobatic loop-the-loop?
Can you spot the three people in the crowd wearing red hats?

Demolition Site

Bang! Crash! Boom! The demolition workers have been busy today! Add diggers and piles of rubble ready to be scooped up and taken away.

Fun in the Fields

It's harvest time. Fill the fields with a combine harvester, tractors, bales of hay, and crops.

The birds are trying to eat the corn! How many can you see?

Match the Shadows

Draw lines to match each farm vehicle with its shadow.

Add a bale of hay for each shadow you match.

Big Tractor Coloring

Color in the big tractor. Draw yourself in the driver's seat.

Water Sports

Add lots of people trying different water sports on the lake. Some like to ride in speedboats and on jet skis. Some like to waterski or parasail.

Which water sport would you like to try?

Ambulance Maze

The ambulance needs to get to the hospital fast! Can you find your way through the maze as quickly as possible?

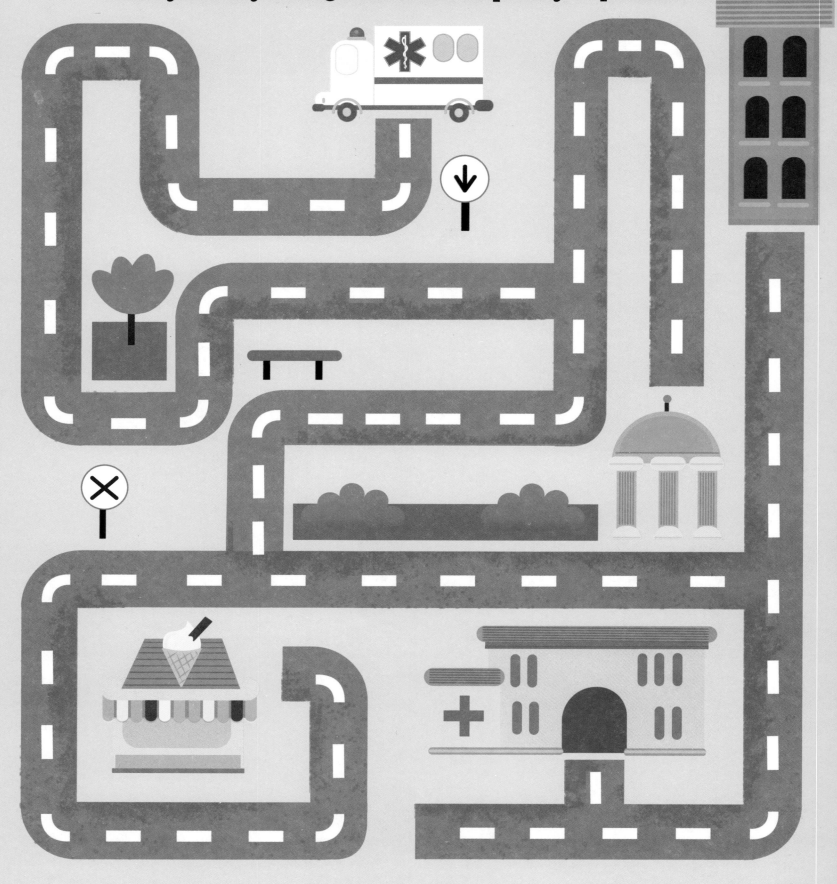

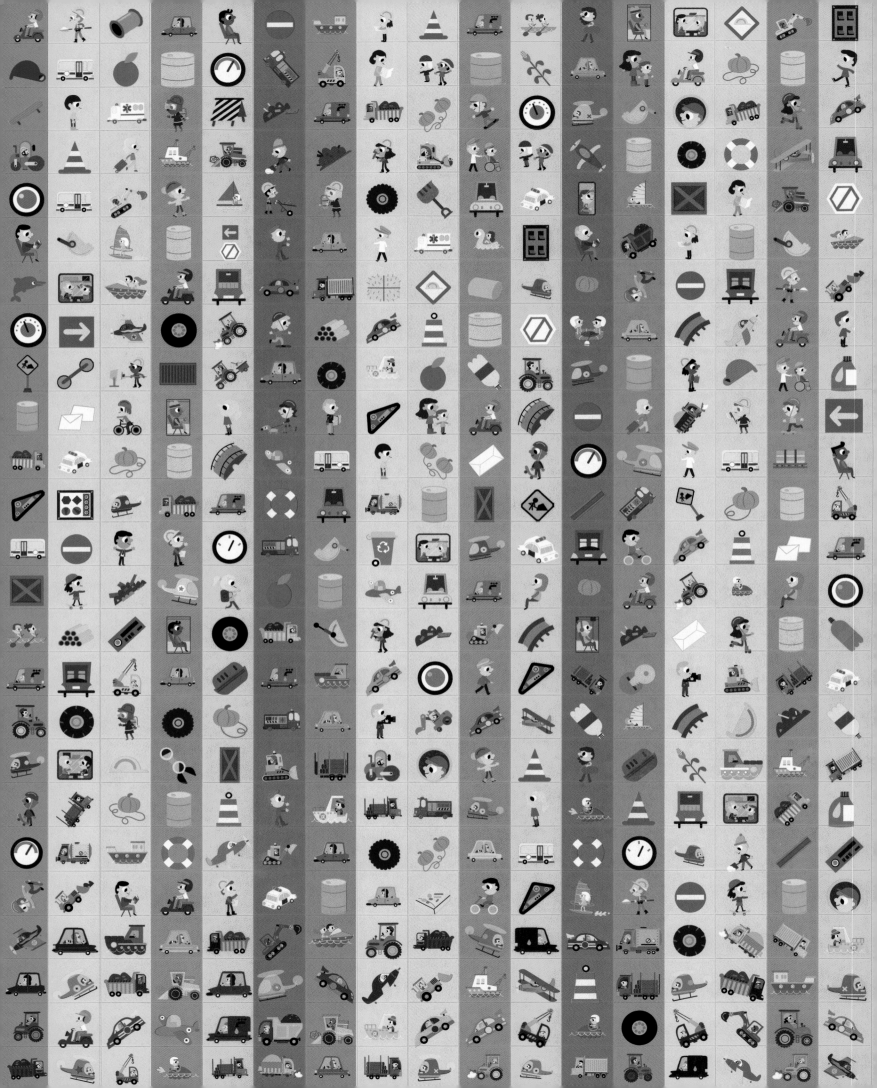

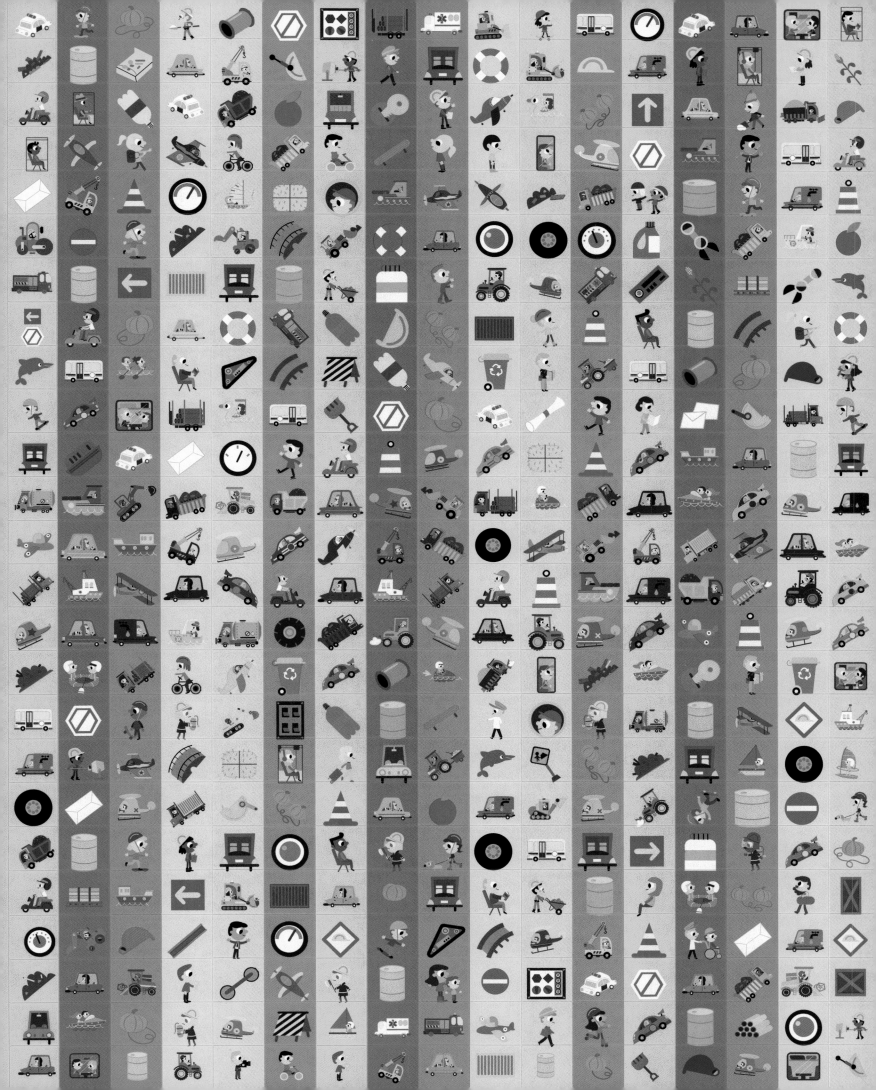

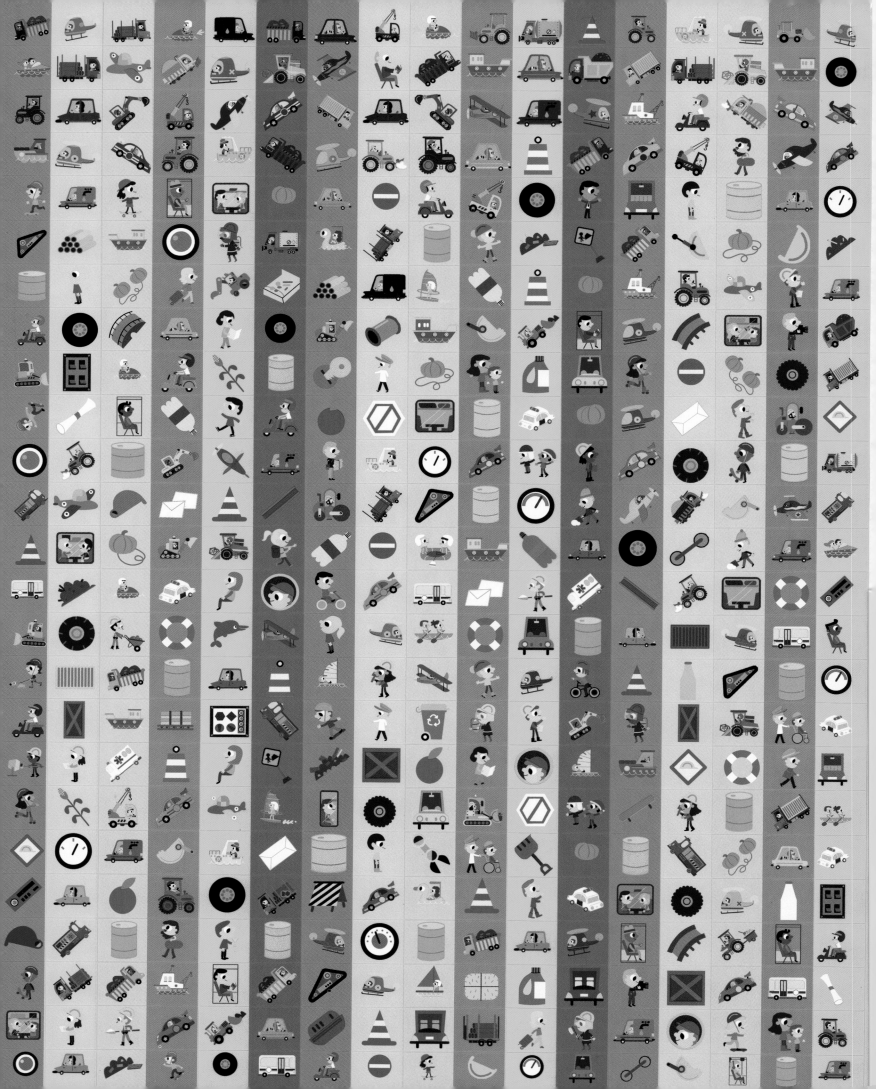

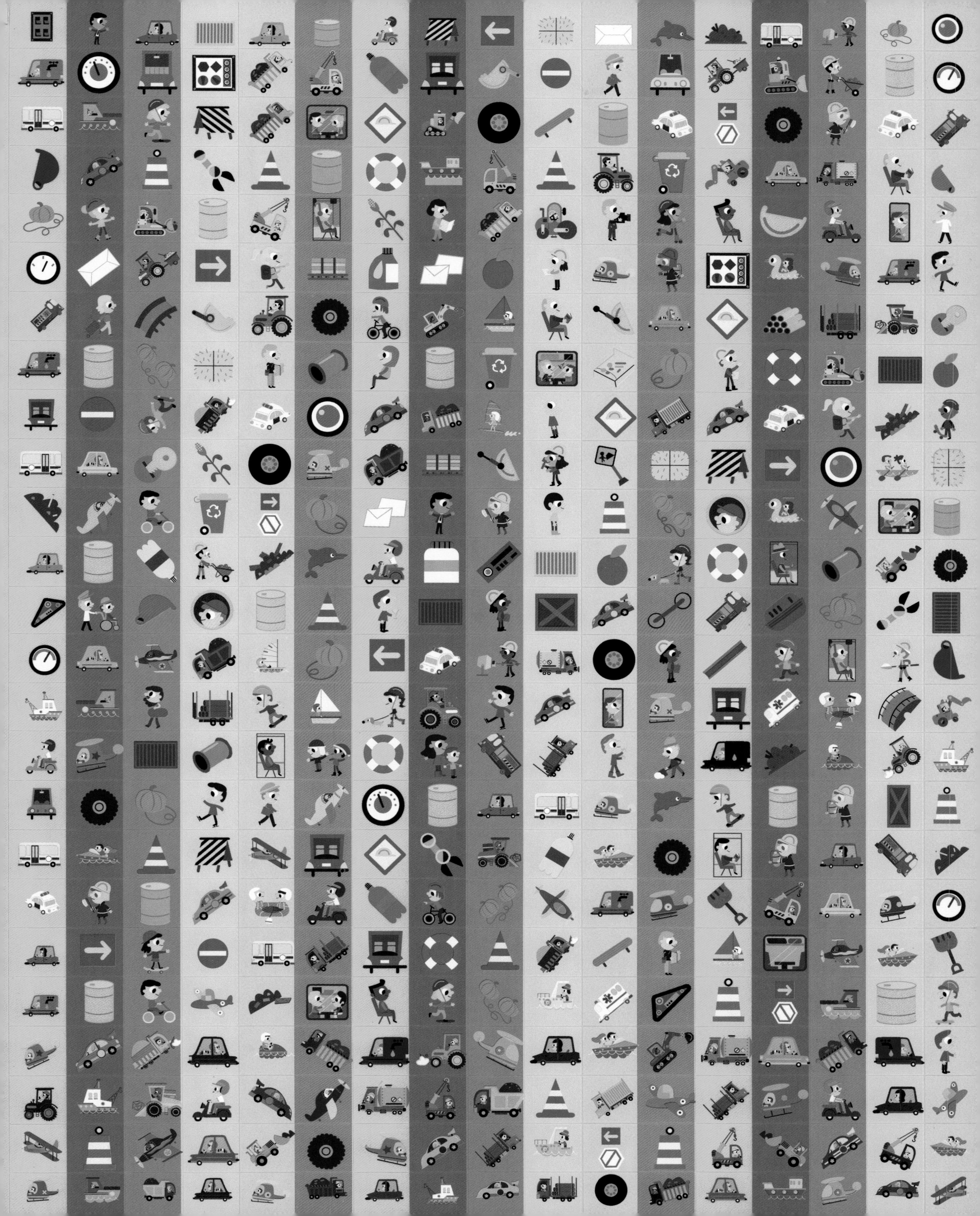

Stop! Police!

The red car is driving too fast down a busy highway. Add police cars chasing the car, but watch out for other traffic!

POLICE

POLICE

How many green cars are on the highway?

Forest Fire! Help!

Help! There's a fire in the woods! Use your stickers to add the fire crew putting the fire out.

Can you see what might have started the fire?

Train Station

The train is about to leave the station. Fill the platform with passengers, and add windows and wheels to the passenger cars with your stickers.

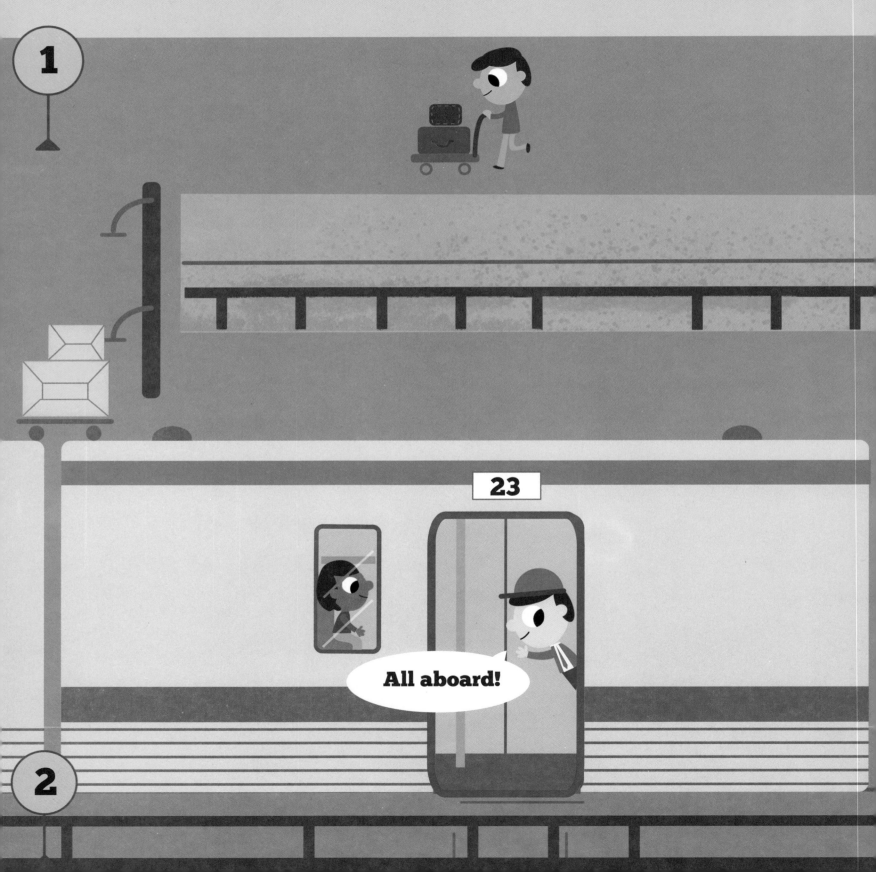

Can you see the passenger with the big green suitcase?

Snowy Day

Help clear the streets of snow with more snowplows so that people can get moving.

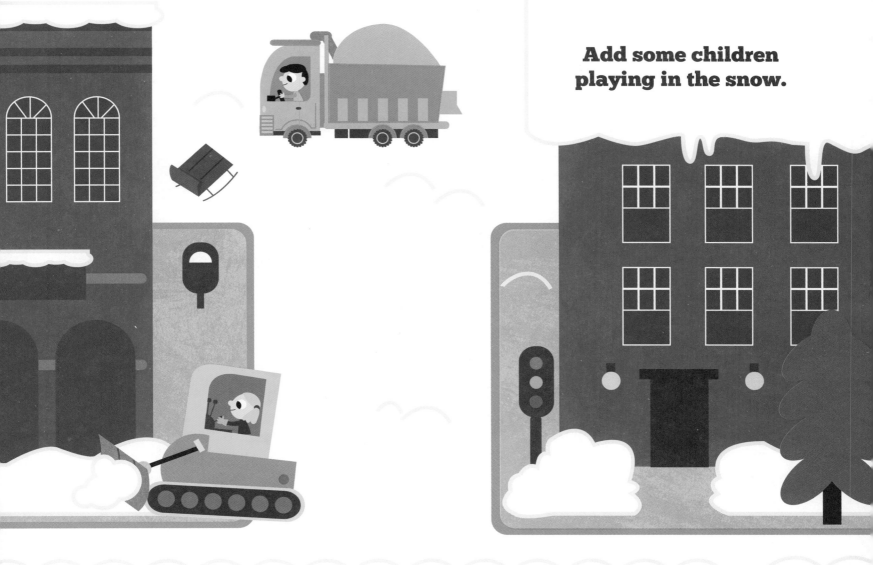

Add some children playing in the snow.

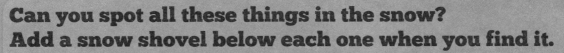

Can you spot all these things in the snow?
Add a snow shovel below each one when you find it.

Mega Mine

Work never stops at the mine. Each vehicle has its own job to do—digging, scooping, and moving. Add dump trucks to help move earth and rocks away.

Coal Truck Coloring

Color in the dump truck to help the miners get the job done.

Cruise Ship

Hop aboard! The round-the-world cruise is about to set sail. Can you add more lifeboats before it leaves the port?

Count all the
seabirds in the scene.
How many did
you spot?

Draw your smiling
face in the porthole!

Recycling Run

It's recycling collection day. Drive past all the containers
to pick them up, then get to the recycling center.

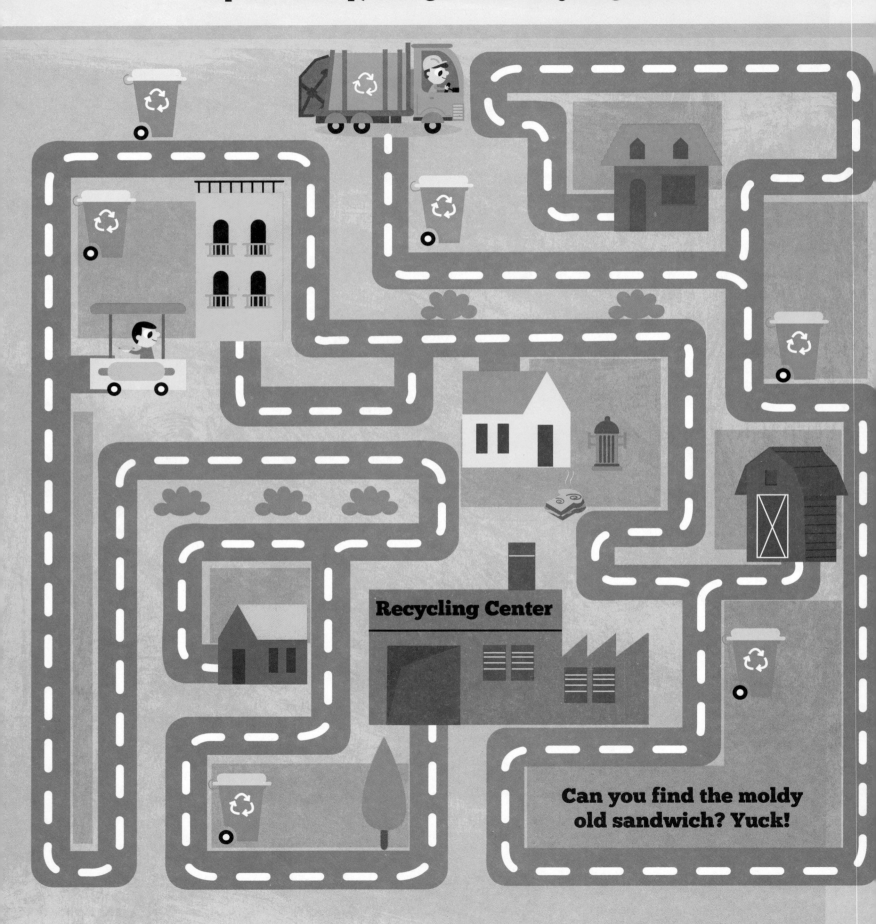

Recycling Center

**Can you find the moldy
old sandwich? Yuck!**

Sort the Trash

Help the workers put the recyclables into the different containers with your stickers.

Timber Trucks

The timber company needs to get more logs to its factory. Add trucks filled with logs to the roads.

Oh, no! All the bridges over the river are missing. Build bridges for the trucks with your stickers.

Scootering and Skating

It's busy in the skatepark today. Add lots of children scootering, riding, skating, and zooming around!

Find the matching pair
of bicycles and the matching
pair of scooters.

Building Site

A new school is being built in the city. Add cement mixers ready to pour the foundations and some builders to get the job done.

One of the builders
has lost his hard hat.
Can you find it
for him?

Helicopter Game

These helicopters can't remember where to land. Follow the line from each helicopter to its helipad.

Add a matching helicopter sticker on each helipad to land it.

Chopper Trouble

Can you spot 5 differences between these two pictures?

Add a helicopter sticker here each time you spot a difference.

Answers: Ear protectors, joystick position, star, door window, rear rotor.

Let's Go Racing!

Get your racing cars on the move and fill up the track with zooming engines! **GO, GO, GO!**

**Can you find
the cameraperson
filming the race?**

Load the Crane

This crane has arrived on-site ready to lift and move crates, containers, and more.